The Premier Edition of

The Tooth Fairy Legend:
The Touch of Kindness

includes the double CD set
of the narrated story and
fully-orchestrated songs
from the family musical.

Order yours today at your
local book/music store
or online at
www.thetouchofkindness.com.

5/12/02

This Book Donated to the
Cardington Public Library
From
Wilma Long Kinsell
& Willis Long
Author a former local
resident.

The Tooth Fairy Legend:
The Touch of Kindness

by
John Arthur Long
and
Chet Meyer

45407
RAC

Illustrations by Nadine Zenobi

The Tooth Fairy Legend: The Touch of Kindness © 2002 by John Arthur Long & Chet Meyer

Published by:
L & M Creations
PO Box 415
Round Top, New York 12473

ISBN: 0-9710749-0-9

First L & M Creations Printing, March 2002

Book copyright 2002 by John Arthur Long and Chet Meyer
Original concept book copyright 1968
Illustrations copyright 2002 by Nadine Zenobi

Printed in the U. S. A.

www.thetouchofkindness.com

The Tooth Fairy Legend:
The Touch of Kindness
A Secret Plan

Piper Noble had a plan. He had lost teeth before, but every time he placed a tooth under his pillow, it had been replaced by a shiny new coin without his seeing so much as a wing of the Tooth Fairy. He lifted an eyelid and checked the string that was attached to his left pinkie. There was just enough moonlight for him to see the string that ran past his ear and under the pillow. Now, even if he fell asleep, the tiny tug of the string on his little finger would awaken him, and he could see whoever it was who came to exchange money for secondhand teeth.

He waited. Sometimes, he didn't know whether he was really asleep or just pretending, and he had to wriggle his nose to make sure. Then it happened! A large gumdrop ran to the top of the blanket and looked him right in the face. Soon, it ran off and disappeared. The Tooth Fairy doesn't look like a gumdrop, does she? Piper lay there, still pretending to be asleep, peeking cautiously with his eyes half-open. He heard a scuffling just below the open window. A lumpy shadow was climbing the Venetian blind cord hand over hand. It had the body of a gigantic gumdrop. But its body was really its face, too! And in the middle of its face was a big bulb of a nose. Below the nose was a smiling orange section of a mouth. And above, one on each side of the nose, were silvery, shining eyes like large coins — just like the ones that were always left under his pillow in exchange for his teeth!

Apparently, the gumdrop did not know Piper was awake, because it turned and signaled out the window, waving its tiny arms and making a scratchy, muffled call that brought Piper's half-closed eyes wide open.

"Ack, Ack!" said the gumdrop, and in through the window flew one of the most beautiful sights Piper Noble had ever seen.

The Tooth Fairy? It had to be! Piper couldn't believe it, but there she was, standing in his bedroom talking to a lumpy stick man.

Meeting The Tooth Fairy

"Is he asleep?" she whispered. Piper slammed his eyes shut just as they looked at him.

"Ack!" came the answer, and Piper wanted so much to giggle that he almost couldn't stand it. So he held his breath, and lay there silent and happy, not wanting to scare them away.

The Tooth Fairy flew over to Piper's bed, while her companion posted himself on the window sill like a watchful sentry. Piper felt his pillow being gently lifted, as he awaited the tug from the string on his finger.

"Psst, hey, Ack, come look at this," said the Tooth Fairy. "This tooth is boobytrapped with a string." Ack left the window, swung to the floor and ran to the bedside. When he saw the string, he hopped happily up and down. "This boy Piper is definitely a smart young man," she whispered to Ack. When she turned back to the bed,

Piper's big blue eyes were wide open.

"Hi!" he said, "I'm Piper Noble. Are you really the Tooth Fairy?"

The Tooth Fairy turned to her little lookout. "I think we're in trouble again, Ack," she said. "Some scout you are. I thought you said he was asleep. He's not only very smart, he's very awake! Let's get out of here!"

Piper sat up in bed quickly and scrambled to his knees. "No, wait, please, I won't tell, honest. Besides, I've already seen you, so you might as well stay and talk to me for a minute. And look, you even forgot my tooth!"

Ack sneaked closer to the bed and then leaped up, trying to grab the tooth. But Piper was too fast for him. He pulled it away just in time and held it high in the air.

"Oh, no you don't! If I give you this tooth, you'll leave. I'll make a deal with you. If you talk to me for just five minutes, I'll give you this tooth...and all the other ones that come out for nothing. And I won't tell anyone at all. Cross my heart. Okay?"

The Tooth Fairy went over to Ack and picked him up off the floor. They both sat on the bed, and Piper knew that he was the luckiest person in the world.

However, when the Tooth Fairy spoke, she sounded kind of upset. "Now, listen,

Piper, I'm probably in big trouble already, but if you ever say anything, then for sure...."

"LITTLE WINGS! What on Earth do you think you're doing?"

The Tooth Fairy scrunched up her shoulders and wrapped her wings over her ears. Ack jumped down to the floor and hid under the bed. Piper took one look at the shadowy figure in the window and dove under the covers. Now he was scared. He peeked out through a fold in the sheets and saw a lady coming straight towards the bed.

"Now, Auntie Flossie," said Little Wings, "before you get all excited...."

"There will be no explanations," replied Auntie Flossie. "You and that detestable little Sniffen of yours are leaving this instant. And let's hope that this lad can be trusted to keep this bungled visit a secret."

"I can," cried Piper, throwing off the covers. "I crossed my heart and everything." At that moment the Sniffen tried to sneak out from under the bed, tripped over Auntie Flossie's foot, and went rolling across the floor.

"You, you little pest, are probably the cause of this entire mess," said Auntie Flossie, pointing at the small creature's large nose. Little Wings patted the blanket beside her, and Ack skipped over and jumped up onto the bed.

Piper leaned over to the Tooth Fairy. "What's that?" he whispered, pointing to Ack.

"Who, him?" Little Wings said, smiling. "That's Ack. He's my...."

(SONG: "The Sniffen Song")

"And it's my guess," Auntie Flossie continued, "that he is the reason we are all in this present fix. Isn't that right, Little Wings?"

"But it wasn't his fault this time," the Tooth Fairy protested.

"How else do you explain getting caught?"

Piper grabbed the string from where it lay on the blanket and held it out. "I did that," he grinned. "I set a boobytrap. Don't hurt them."

"I don't want to hurt Little Wings, young man. Or anyone else, for that matter. But we have a job to do, and I must make sure it's done properly."

"Oh, I know," said Piper. "You have to collect teeth from kids like me who lose them."

"Yes, for the most part that is the case," answered Auntie Flossie. "But now our job is much more difficult — and much more important — than usual."

"It is?" Little Wings questioned.

"Why?" said Piper.

"It's Starling Patch, Little Wings." The Tooth Fairy looked surprised, shocked and scared all at once. The Sniffen began to shake with fear. "Because of his hate, the Isle of Kindness is slowly being destroyed. It's becoming a wasteland of ice. And the Eternal Fire is very nearly out!"

"Oh, no. It's all my fault, Auntie Flossie," cried Little Wings.

"No, we're all to blame. We should have realized that the only way to deal with hate is to destroy it in the very beginning, or it will grow to destroy everything in the end."

"I don't understand," Piper said softly.

"I'm sorry, Piper, but there are secrets that no one on Earth must ever know. We have to go now."

Little Wings and Ack sadly waved goodbye, and headed towards the window.

"But isn't there anything I can do to help?" Piper pleaded.

"No, we have to find a way to melt all the ice that's threatening our home, and that's too much to ask of even a very brave and clever boy."

"Well, you said you had a fire. Why don't you use that before it goes out?"

"Let's just say the fire I'm talking about doesn't melt ice. Okay?"

"Then build a regular ice-melting fire like people do to keep warm at the skating pond."

Auntie Flossie's eyebrows raised. "Do you know how to build one of those ice-melting fires?"

Piper grinned. "Sure. Anyone can! I saw a great way to do it on a T.V. science show. You don't need matches or anything."

Auntie Flossie was silent for a moment. Then she looked from Piper to Little Wings and back again. "You know, it just might work! Piper, if I knew of any other way to solve our problem, I would not do this. But if you can show us how to melt that ice and save our Home-Fire, it's worth breaking the rules. Will you come back with us and try?"

"Sure. Where are we going?"

"To the Isle of Kindness that I mentioned before. Now hurry up, we must leave immediately. And be certain you take all we'll need!"

Piper's heart leaped in his chest with excitement. It was unbelievable! They were going to take him with them to their home! He ran behind his bed to change.

"How long will we be gone?" he asked, pulling on his clothes.

"Don't worry," Auntie Flossie answered him. "Time is different for us. When you return, it won't even seem like you've been gone at all."

"I can get what we need for the fire anywhere," Piper said as he hopped out on one foot from behind his bed, tying his shoelace. "Let's go."

Riding A Moonbeam

Little Wings flew through the window, and the others climbed out onto the moonlit lawn after her.

"Which way do we go?" asked Piper.

"That way," said Little Wings, pointing up into the night sky.

"That way?" asked Piper. "How do we do that?"

"On a moonbeam, of course," answered Auntie Flossie, flashing one of her special understanding smiles. "You'll be able to come with us because we know how to use the moon's magnetic energy. You'll see."

"You mean that the moon's forces can move us like it does the waves of the ocean?"

"Very much like that, Piper," Auntie Flossie said. "Remember what happens if you leave a dish of water

outside on a sunny day?"

"Yeah! The water disappears because it gets evaporated by the sun's heat."

"That's right. And in much the same way we can be...well, not evaporated, but... transported by the magnetic forces of the moon. It's not as magical as it may sound, Piper. Everything in the universe is interconnected in more ways than anyone can possibly imagine."

The four joined hands and formed a circle. When the other three closed their eyes and took long, deep relaxing breaths, lifting their faces toward the sparkling heavens above them, Piper tried to do the same, but he couldn't resist peeking.

At first, nothing happened. Then Auntie Flossie sang a clear, high-pitched musical tone, and suddenly, Piper saw throbbing golden rays of light appear above the heads of each of his three new friends and surround them in a glowing illumination. With the golden light, he felt a shimmering warmth gathering around him.

When Little Wings harmonized with Auntie Flossie, a wonderful powder blue color appeared in an aura of pulsating haze around each of their bodies. Then glowing lights of every color of the rainbow appeared to surround each body beyond the blue. And finally, a brilliant white star-shaped sparkle of illumination ignited at the center of each of them, and with the softness of an angel's touch, a gentle force tugged at him, pulling him upward.

Then, very slowly, they all began to float, bouncingly at first, then, like bubbles on a summer breeze. Piper held on tightly and closed his eyes. A flash of fear snaked up his spine, but he heard a reassuring "Ack" beside him.

(SONG: "You Can Ride On a Moonbeam")

"You can open your eyes now. I thought you'd want to see the neighborhood before it got too small for you to recognize anything."

"Wow, it worked. We really are flying."

"Of course."

"How will we be able to breathe? We're going into space."

"Oh, don't worry, Piper. There are things in the moonbeam that will protect you and bring you back home again in No Time. Listen."

Below, Piper saw all his friends' houses, but they were the size of the plastic buildings on his train set board. Ahead, extending into the sky before them as they rose

was a huge, glowing beam of pulsating light. Piper glanced behind him again, but he lost sight of the whole street as his head went into a low cloud.

Piper smiled and turned his head upwards. "It's so beautiful. Can anyone do this?"

Auntie Flossie's eyes radiated sympathetic understanding. "No, it's only because you are with us that you can ride a moonbeam. You see, your world is not yet ready to be given this kind of knowledge and power. It will only happen when there is enough Kindness given off by people to overcome the powers of hate and jealousy that exist on Earth."

"We're going to hit the moon!"

"No, we're not. We're going to go right past it and through the sky."

"Oh, I know we're going through the sky now."

"No, I mean we really are going to go through the sky. I believe your scientists call the passage a black hole in space. Piper, the sky is like a painting, and we live on the other side. Hold tight..., here we go."

At that moment, the group was pulled strongly towards a swirl of stars. Flashes of multi-colored light and harmonious melodies were all around them, and Piper suddenly understood. At this magical spot, this mysterious hole in space, the sky opened to them and they were indeed going through it to the Isle of Kindness, a very important fire that doesn't melt ice, and Starling Patch, whoever he was.

The Isle Of Kindness

Below them the Isle hung in mists of changing colors, some of which Piper couldn't even name. It was round like a pie tin, but from the outer edges almost to the center it was ragged and white from the crust of ice. Little Wings noticed Piper's curiosity, and flew over to him.

"This is the Isle of Kindness," she began, "but it didn't always have all that ice around it. That must be Starling's work. He lives at the outer edge of the Isle because he was banished from the center when we noticed that the Eternal Fire shrank back whenever he came near it. There's the Fire, right down there." Below, tongues of silver and gold flames stretched up weakly from the middle of a ring of ice.

Balanced above the Fire was a gigantic beam. It looked solid, but Piper knew it was some strange kind of light, both delicate and strong at the same time. One arm of it reached out ahead of them into and through the wispy flashes of color at the edge of the opposite side of the Isle. The other arm extended below and behind them like a long highway or landing field.

"What is that?" Piper asked, pointing at the beam.

Auntie Flossie glowed with pride. "That is the supreme secret of the universe, Piper. It is called the Celestial Balance, and without it, the universe would spin out of control. The Eternal Fire keeps the Balance in place. And now I will explain why Tooth Fairies collect teeth from under the pillows of little children. You see, one arm of the Celestial Balance follows the path we just took, and is connected to the Earth. The other arm runs past the Isle and far off into space on this side of the sky."

Suddenly, Piper knew! "What's at the other end?" he asked eagerly.

Auntie Flossie's smile broadened. "From the look on your face, I think you already know."

Piper giggled. "It's teeth, isn't it? THE TEETH BALANCE THE UNIVERSE!"

Auntie Flossie nodded happily. "Now let me tell you exactly how it all works. You see, it's actually the children of the world who keep everything from getting unbalanced. When they lose their teeth, as you know, they place them under their pillows, and Tooth Fairies like Little Wings pick them up at night and bring them here to the Isle of Kindness. Then, special workers, called Metrognomes, load them onto the Celestial Balance's powerful moving beam of light. At the far end of the arm of the beam, the teeth are deposited into a huge container, where they act as a counter-balance to the weight of the Earth."

Piper broke in excitedly. "And as more children are born, you need more teeth in the container to balance us all, right?"

"Right. If you just give a little of yourself now and then, like a tooth when you're young, everyone will benefit. When you're older, you can be kind to others and give the gift of life, so that other children can take their turns helping to keep everything in balance."

They landed near the Eternal Fire.

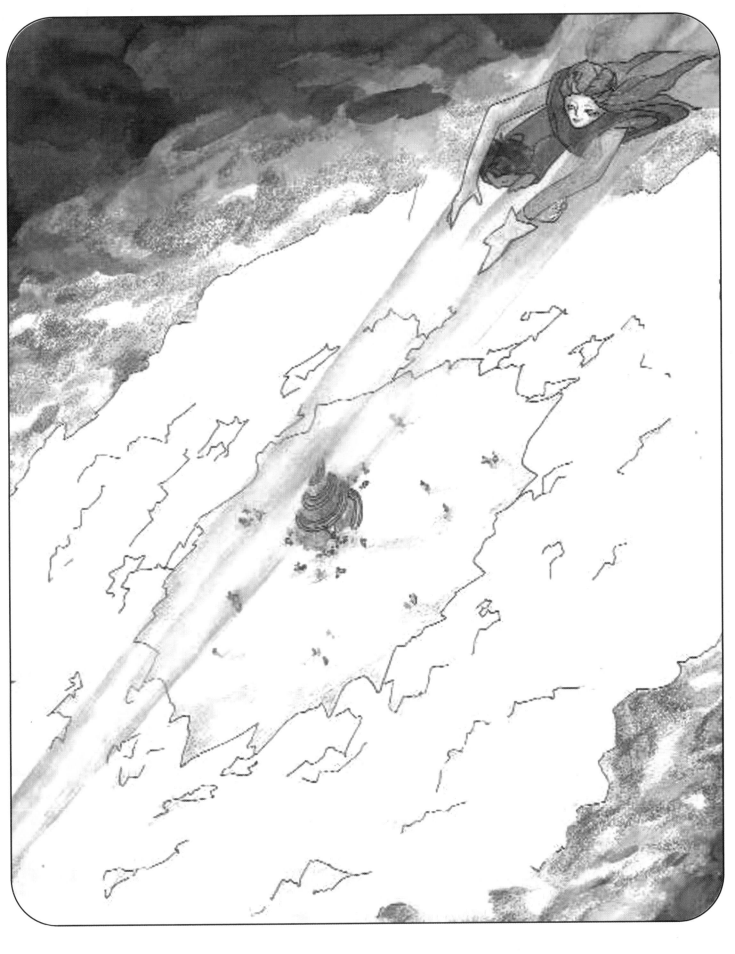

Searching For Wood

There were workers of all sizes around the unusually beautiful metallic flames. Some workers were skinny, some fat. Some were tall, some short. Some were lifting teeth and putting them onto the strip of moving light at the top of the beam. Some were filling bottles at the base of the Fire.

Ack hopped around watching what the workers were doing, getting in their way most of the time. He hopped up onto the moving beam of light, jolted forward, and slammed right into a round Metrognome who had just leaned over to deposit another pouchful of teeth.

"Ah, you," he roared. "Get out of here!" The worker grabbed Ack and dropped him to the ground. "Wherever you go, you get into trouble."

Ack ran to Little Wings' side, passing a large Metrognome who looked up from his work station and refocused his rapidly blinking eyes on Ack. He glared over at Little Wings. "One of these days, I'm going to throw that miserable Sniffen of yours out into the Consuming Colors, so he'll vanish forever!"

Auntie Flossie cleared her throat, bringing the muscular Metrognome to attention. "Careful, Blinker," she said, "or you'll put out the Fire with your gruff talk...before Starling Patch has a chance to."

"Uh, Sorry Ma'am, I was just trying to get my job done." Blinker was built like a blacksmith. Piper thought he could feel the ground shake when Blinker spoke because his voice was so deep and strong. His eyes constantly batted up and down, as if winking them both at once. "Glad you're back, Ma'am," Blinker said. "Things are getting pretty rough, and I guess that's why I'm so upset. That blasted Starling's been showing up everywhere. I've had to post lookouts all over the place. We're doing our best, but I'm powerful worried."

Auntie Flossie nodded. "I understand, Blinker, but I think I may have a solution."

"What?" exclaimed the huge Metrognome.

She motioned for Piper to come forward. "Blinker, this is Piper Noble. Piper, this is Blinker, the foreman of the Metrognomes."

Blinker blinked, smiled, and reached out his huge hand.

"Pleased to meet ya, Diaper," Blinker boomed as he and Piper shook hands.

Ack acked in disapproval, and Little Wings said, "No, Blinker, that's PIPER...PIPER Noble."

"I thought it was Diaper, 'cause he's so little. Well, I'm still pleased to meet ya. Are you the solution?"

"Indeed he is," Auntie Flossie stated emphatically. "Piper can show us how to build the kind of fire that melts ice."

"Excellent," said Blinker, grinning broadly. "What do you need to start one of these fires?"

"Just some wood," Piper replied.

"Uh, wood? What's wood?" asked Blinker.

"You know, WOOD... that comes from trees!"

Blinker frowned. "Nope. What's a tree?"

"A TREE, a big plant with leaves and bark and...."

Auntie Flossie kneeled down beside him. "Piper, I thought you said you didn't need to bring anything from home."

"I didn't. I mean, I thought I didn't," Piper said. "You just rub two sticks together. I'll show Blinker how, because I know kids shouldn't play with fire. All I need is wood. It's as sure a thing as the sun coming up every morning."

"It sounds like it," Blinker admitted, his eyelids batting up and down, "but besides not having any wood on the Isle of Kindness, we don't have a sun here, either. Only the Consuming Colors and the Eternal Fire light our way."

"Oh, no," Piper whined in disappointment. "I thought everyone had some kind of wood where they lived. You sure there's not like an old twig or something like that lying around?"

"Nothing like that, Piper," Auntie Flossie said, standing.

"I mean, how was I to know that...well, wood... wood's all over the place, you know...and I never even thought about not having a sun in the sky!"

"Piper, I don't know of anything here that's even remotely like wood," sighed Auntie Flossie.

"Now wait a minute," Blinker said, blinking hard. "Maybe we can find some. Diaper, you better tell us what wood looks like, how it feels and how it smells, 'cause what you call trees and wood we might call something else."

Piper shrugged.

(SONG: "That's Wood")

Piper looked regretfully at Auntie Flossie and Little Wings. "I...I guess I'm not as smart as you thought I was," he said. "I'm afraid I won't be able to build a fire for you."

"It's all right. We still have some time. We'll think of something. I'll have to take you back on my next trip," Auntie Flossie told Piper. "But in the meantime, since he's short-handed, why don't you help Blinker?"

"Don't worry, Piper. At least you tried, and none of us has done any better," Little Wings said as she turned and followed after Auntie Flossie.

"Come on, Diaper, I'll show you around," Blinker said, and he walked around the base of the Eternal Fire.

Blinker Explains

"Blinker," Piper said, hurrying after the lumbering Metrognome, "I feel terrible about not being able to help."

"Well, think how Little Wings feels! In a way, this whole Starling thing was her fault," Blinker said.

"Who is Starling, anyway?"

"Well, he used to be one of my most trusted Metrognomes, but he wasn't happy being what he was. He wanted to be a Tooth Fairy! Of course, that was impossible! I mean, you're either a Metrognome or a Tooth Fairy or a Sniffen, or...yeah, or a Little Person like you, but you can't change that. You just have to be the best Metrognome or Tooth Fairy or Little Person that you possibly can. Starling, however, wasn't satisfied with that. He envied the life of a Tooth Fairy so much that he started brooding about it and working less and less. Pretty soon, his envy turned to hate, and that's when we started having trouble with the Fire."

"But I still don't understand. Why is this fire so special?"

"Diaper, this fire is one of the most unique elements in the universe. You see, the

Eternal Fire is fed by love and understanding. That's its fuel. Just as your kind of fire uses that, uh...wood, this one is most alive and beautiful when those around it are good. In return, it gives off Kindness, just as your type of fire would give off heat."

"What happens when there are bad people around the fire?"

"It shrinks back and starts to die, and that's what happened when Starling came close. And it only happened when he was on Fire detail or bottle pickup."

"So, what did you do?"

"Well, we had a meeting. Everyone came to it. We decided to throw Starling Patch into the Consuming Colors, and get rid of him forever." Blinker looked at Piper straight in the eyes. "Anyone who goes out there without riding a moonbeam along the exact path you took vanishes forever! Anyway, we voted, and the majority opinion was that Starling should be consumed by the Colors as a public menace and a threat to the Fire. We formed a detail, and Starling took off quick as he could. He was one scared Metrognome. We chased him all over the island. Ack was hopping about and acking, Metrognomes were bumping into one another... it was a real horrible sight. One time, Patch jumped over the Fire to get away from us and we all lost our breath 'cause it nearly went out. Then, he hopped up onto the conveyor belt and tried to ride it away from us. But I quickly threw it into reverse, and soon we had him in hand.

"We carried him above our heads, holding on to him tightly. And that wasn't easy. He sure was kicking. We carried him over to the edge of the island. In fact, it was right over there. Yes, right there! And I shouted on the count of three we'd throw him over. One: they swung him back between them by his hands and feet. Two: they swung him harder, and all the time Starling was yelling and screaming how he hated us and how he'd get even with us all, Tooth Fairies included. Just as I was about to yell, 'THREE,' that brat of a Sniffen jumped on my back and put both hands over my mouth. I couldn't say a word. At the same time, Little Wings flew over and stood right on the edge of the island in front of us. 'Stop,' she yelled. That's when we saw she was crying. 'No matter how bad a person is,' she said, 'you shouldn't kill him. That makes you as bad as he is. I think we should just banish Starling so he won't be allowed to come near the Fire again.' Well, Little Wings can be pretty persuasive, even when she's not crying."

Piper watched intently as Blinker's eyelids flipped up and down faster than ever. The Consuming Colors exploded in flashes of glowing multi-colored light around them, and the Metrognome's expression filled with emotion as he continued his story. "So I told the Metrognomes to put Starling down and we took a revote. Everyone decided that banishment was a better idea. Starling was sentenced to the edge of the island, and we told him that if he ever left there, we'd throw him over for sure. Everyone backed away from him, and he looked at us, long and hard. Diaper, he had the meanest look on his face I ever saw or ever hope to see. He stared for a long time like that and then he started screaming and jumping up and down like he'd gone crazy. 'I hate you, I hate you,' he cried, and he swore he'd make us pay. And then he left, spitting at us. We never saw him again until the ice started forming and moving in toward the Fire. As his hate grew, of course, so did the ice," Blinker continued, sadly. "Now he hates us so much, he's going to destroy us all by choking the Fire to death. When the Eternal Fire goes out, everything down below will spin out of control. Nobody can survive a disaster like that!"

"But why didn't you all go out and get him when the ice first appeared?"

"Come here," Blinker said, "I'll show ya." He walked Piper over to the rim of the ice, pointing out over the wide white horizon. "You see that twisted form on the ice out there?"

"Yeah! It looks like a tree!"

"That's no tree, Diaper. That's Tapper — best Bottler I ever had, and one of our most courageous Metrognomes. Tapper saw Starling skulking around on the other side of that huge icicle. And when he started lobbing ice cubes at the Fire, Tapper ran out onto the ice to grab him, but it was a cruel trap. Tapper froze solid. Starling was testing his power, and from that time on we knew that any Metrognome who touches that ice will freeze for sure. So, you see, we're really in a fine fix, and it looks like nobody can help. We have all shifts on overtime now, we're so busy tending the Fire and filling the bottles."

"What bottles, Blinker?"

"Come over here to the other side of the Fire, and I'll show you."

Bottles Of Kindness

As Piper followed Blinker around the Fire's base, he saw Metrognomes feverishly filling and capping bottles. But Piper didn't know how the Metrognomes knew when the bottles were full because all the containers in the stacks of cases looked empty. "Blinker, is there anything in those bottles?" Piper asked.

"Of course. We never waste a bottle around here. In fact, we try not to waste anything."

"Well, then why does it look like there's nothing in them?"

"Huh, well, I don't know. Let me think for a minute. What color is love where you come from, Diaper?"

"Color? I don't know. It doesn't have a color!"

Blinker nodded with assurance. "That's it, then. Things like love and happiness and Kindness, they don't have any colors to people where you come from."

Piper squinted and looked as hard as he could at the bottles. "Well, what's in them, anyway?"

"Diaper, those bottles are filled with concentrated Kindness, the purest form of goodness in the universe."

"What kindness?"

"The Kindness that clings to teeth when they're given out of love to the Tooth Fairies by little children."

"You mean that kindness hangs onto things when you touch them?"

"If you're feeling kind at the time, yes. And, you can pass on Kindness that way, too. If you give a present to someone because you like him or her, Kindness goes along with the gift. It's the same way with teeth. I guess the reason you can't see it is that as long as there's Kindness in people, it doesn't matter what the color is!"

"What do you do with the bottles after they're filled?"

"We ship them down to Earth. You know, folks can be pretty mean to one another down there. Sometimes they need a little help."

"Then when kids like me give their teeth to the Tooth Fairy...WOW! We not only help keep everything in balance, we help spread kindness throughout the world, don't we?"

"Yup. Makes kids just a little more important than you thought, doesn't it?"

"Boy, if I'd known that, I never would have worried when I started losing my teeth."

"Why, sure. It's all right if your teeth fall out. As any Metrognome will tell you, you've got nothing to worry about.

(SONG: "It's All Right If Your Teeth Fall Out")

"Now, I better stop gabbing and get back to work. You just make yourself at home, Diaper."

"Okay. Thanks, Blinker," Piper said as he watched the big Metrognome climb up towards the light beam. Then, he sat down near the base of the Fire, and as he watched the Metrognomes work, Piper thought about all that Blinker had told him.

Starling Patch

"Hi, Piper," said Little Wings. Piper looked sideways and felt his heart jump a bit. There she was, looking as cute as the first time he saw her fly through his window. Ack was holding her hand.

"Hi, Little Wings," Piper replied, jumping to his feet. "I was just sitting here thinking about Starling Patch and all the trouble he's causing. I wish there were something I could...." Suddenly, a blurry movement out on the ice snagged Piper's attention. "LITTLE WINGS, WHAT'S THAT?"

As Little Wings shielded her eyes and peered out at the icy area that Piper was watching, Ack bounced up and down excitedly and ran behind the Tooth Fairy's legs to hide. The three of them heard an evil laugh. And then they saw something ragged and horrible skidding across the ice.

"There's only one thing that could be, Piper," said Little Wings in a shaky voice. "Starling Patch!"

"Wh... wh... what should we do?" asked Piper. "I think we better warn Blinker. Oh, but that won't do any good, 'cause he'll only freeze if he goes out there. But, maybe...."

Piper stopped talking and thought very hard. Just because Metrognomes froze when they touched the ice didn't mean that he would. Or that Little Wings or Ack would,

either! He looked at his two friends. If it didn't work, they'd be frozen statues forever. But time was running out. There was no time to be afraid. There was only time left to be brave.

"But...but, maybe what?" said the Tooth Fairy.

"Little Wings, maybe WE won't freeze if we go after Starling. And I feel bad about not being able to start that fire."

"And it's all my fault that Starling's still around to cause trouble," said Little Wings. Ack shook his head back and forth. "Okay, Ack, you can stay here, but we're going."

"Let's go!" Piper took Little Wings' hand, swallowed hard, and they started towards the edge of the ice. Behind them they heard "acks" that seemed to beg them to stop. They were scared.

"It's now or never," said Piper, and he and Little Wings took a deep breath, closed their eyes, and each placed a trembling foot onto the frigid floor of Starling's kingdom of hate.

As Piper's foot touched the ice, he felt the coldest possible cold shoot through his body. Was he frozen? He tried to shake an arm. It moved. He tried the other one. That one moved, too. He sure was cold, but he wasn't frozen. He turned to Little Wings. She looked fine too, but her thin wings were frosted over.

"Are you okay?" asked Piper.

"Well, I can't fly, but I can still move around." Then they heard an "ack" at their feet. There, hopping around next to them was a shivering Sniffen.

"Atta boy, Ack," said Piper.

"Oh, I knew you couldn't let me go out anywhere without you, Ack. Who'd be my lookout?" said Little Wings.

"Come on," said Piper, "let's surround him. You take one side. I'll take the other. Ack, you go right up the middle and draw his attention."

(SONG: "Never Try to Match Deeds with Starling Patch")

The three split up. Little Wings and Piper circled around on opposite sides. Piper watched Ack run right towards Starling. The little Sniffen didn't even have a chance. Starling was so strong, and Ack so small, that the evil Metrognome simply picked him up like a bowling ball and rolled him back at the Eternal Fire. As Ack rolled, he picked up frost and ice like a snowball does when you make a snowman. He rolled faster and

faster — straight at the Fire.

Now sometimes, when you think everything is going just right, something happens to make everything go wrong. This was one of those times. Little Wings and Piper were almost on top of Patch when, somehow, he suddenly saw both of them.

It should have still been simple to capture him, even though he did see them, two against one and all, but in an instant they were outnumbered. Were they seeing things? What was happening? Where Starling Patch had been standing alone, there were two of him. Then four. Then eight. He was splitting apart right before their eyes.

Then, almost before they knew what was happening, there were so many Patches running around, they couldn't even count them. One grabbed Little Wings roughly. "Piper, help, he's got me!"

Piper knew he had to rescue her, but before he could even move he was surrounded by Starling Patches. They made a circle around him, and they were screaming and snarling and spitting and pointing. They all looked alike — duplicates of evil. Beyond them, Little Wings' cries for help became distant whispers. When Piper could no longer hear her, the circle of Patches suddenly vanished, and he was left alone on the frozen wasteland.

"Oh, no,...Ack,...Little Wings,...we failed."

Cheering Up Ack

"Diaper! Diaper! Come back here before you get hurt," Blinker yelled. Piper saw the powerful Metrognome at the edge of the ice, calling to him.

"I'm coming." He got up and ran back towards the Fire. Piper found Auntie Flossie, Blinker and several Metrognomes waiting for him. Ack was sitting on the ground picking icicles off his body.

"Piper, where's Little Wings?" Auntie Flossie questioned, with a worried look on her face.

"Starling's got her! Hurry up! Come on, we gotta go save her!" Piper ran from Metrognome to Metrognome, pulling on their arms, trying to get them to follow him back out onto the ice.

"Now, hold on! We couldn't go out there, even if we wanted to. I told you that. Now, what happened?" Blinker said, trying to calm Piper down.

"Well, we saw Starling out there and we figured we had a pretty good chance of catching him. We were about to jump him, but he... split apart."

Auntie Flossie gasped and shook her head. "This means that the worst possible thing has finally happened. Evidently, Starling's hate has grown so great that he is able to divide himself."

"How can he do that?" Piper asked.

"Evil breeds evil, Piper," was Auntie Flossie's grim reply .

Blinker spoke up. "Diaper, instead of running out there without thinking, why didn't you come tell me what was going on? You're lucky to be alive, and who knows where Little Wings is or what has happened to her!"

"Piper, you never should have done anything like that without asking permission," Auntie Flossie said. "You know better than that! I brought you up here against my better judgment, and I can see now that I made a bad mistake. As soon as I can arrange it, I'm taking you home. Now go over there and stay with Ack. And keep each other out of any further mischief. Do you understand?"

Piper looked up. He knew he'd only been trying to help. "Yes, Ma'am," he said. Auntie Flossie left, talking to Blinker about how dangerous Starling had become. The

Metrognomes went back to work, and Piper walked sadly over to the Sniffen. Ack was shivering slightly.

"Hi, Ack, I'm glad you're safe. I guess we didn't do so well, huh?" For the first time since Piper had met him, the little Sniffen refused to ack. In fact, he didn't even look up. He just stared down at his feet, trembling and crying silently.

"You're worried about Little Wings, aren't you?" Piper said. Ack nodded unhappily. Piper sat down next to his little friend. "Well, I'm worried about her, too. You know, we did the best we could out there." Piper paused, trying to think of a way to cheer the sad little Sniffen up.

(SONG: "The Sniffen Song")

"And there's something else we can do to at least make ourselves useful," Piper said to Ack. "Come on!"

Piper Gets An Idea

Piper helped Ack up and took his hand. They walked over to where Blinker was standing. "Blinker, instead of sitting around doing nothing, we'd like to be on bottle detail."

"Well, maybe you can, but I don't know about him," Blinker said, frowning down at the Sniffen. Immediately, Ack turned around and started to walk away. Piper reached out and pulled him back to his side.

"But, I need him, Blinker. I won't know when the bottles are full. He will!"

Blinker thought for a moment. "Hmmm, you've got a point there. I guess he can be of use to us after all." Blinker blinked, Piper winked and the little Sniffen smiled. "Go relieve Napper. He's sleeping half the time, anyway."

"Thanks, Blinker," Piper yelled, running over towards the Kindness Tap. Ack skipped behind him. "Are you Napper?" Piper asked a Metrognome whose chin rested on his chest.

"Huh, who's there?" said Napper wearily.

"We're here to relieve Napper," Piper answered.

"Well, then you're here to relieve me," Napper replied with one eye shut. "I don't know if I should let you, though." Napper yawned, looking suspiciously at Ack. "Who sent you?"

"Blinker said we could. You can ask him."

"Well, then I guess it's okay. You know how this works?" he asked, pointing to the Tap.

"No, you better show me." All at once, Napper closed the eye that was open and opened the eye that was shut. Then he switched often, always leaving only one eye open. All during the explanation he switched eyes back and forth.

"All you do is take a bottle from here, fill it up at this faucet, put one of those caps in the top, and then put it in one of these shipment cases here. It's simple enough. You got it?"

"Sure, Napper. Thanks."

"Good. Then I guess I'll go grab a little shut-eye."

"Come on, let's get to work, Ack," said Piper.

They bottled slowly at first, but soon they developed a smooth system. Piper filled and the Sniffen acked when each bottle was full. They worked well together. Piper thought about Little Wings. There must be something he could do. Piper's hands worked slower as his mind worked faster. He looked at the bottle he was handing to Ack. Then, as Ack capped that one and watched Piper fill the next bottle, the idea popped into his head. Of course! Bottles of Kindness! Piper smiled and shut off the Tap before the bottle was full.

"Ack, I've got it!" Ack, who was waiting to signal when the bottle was full, didn't know what was happening, and looked up questioningly. "Hurry, hurry, we have to go tell Blinker." Piper ran off, still holding the bottle, motioning for Ack to follow. Ack scratched his head and ran after him. "Blinker, Blinker, I've got it!" shouted Piper.

"Got what, Diaper?"

"I know how to save Little Wings and the Isle of Kindness."

"YOU WHAT?"

"And we can stop Starling Patch. It's very simple."

"I sure hope it's better than that wood idea of yours."

"It is, it is. And this time, I know you have what we need." He handed the half-filled bottle to Blinker.

Blinker looked puzzled as he took the container from Piper. "Kindness? You mean we use Kindness on Starling Patch?" Blinker asked.

Piper nodded. "That's right. And I'll tell you how we can do it."

Little Wings Imprisoned

As her friends planned how to rescue her, Little Wings walked gloomily back and forth, her wings heavy with frost, in Starling Patch's prison of icicles. She couldn't even sit down. Every time she stopped moving, she got so cold she would shake all over. The icicles that surrounded her were high and pointed like the stakes around a wooden fort, but much fatter at the bottom. There was no way out. And it looked as if there was no hope.

(SONG: "Why Can't I Do Anything Right?")

"BECAUSE YOU'RE STUPID!" was the unexpected reply. Little Wings looked up to see two beady eyes peering between the icy bars. "All Tooth Fairies are stupid, and I'm glad I'm not one of them."

"But, Starling, I thought you wanted to be one?" Little Wings answered, wiping a frozen tear from her cheek.

"I thought so too, until I saw what you're really like. Nobody was ever nice to me. I hate little kids. They don't even know I exist. I hate Tooth Fairies 'cause they get all the glory. And I hate Kindness." Starling started jumping up and down like a madman. Faster and faster he jumped, screeching, "I hate you, I hate you, I hate you." And when he wasn't screaming, he was spitting. But it was so cold, his spit froze in midair, hitting Little Wings like hailstones.

"Starling, you're wrong. We all play a small, but very important part in the universe. The Tooth Fairies couldn't do their job at all if it weren't for Metrognomes and Auntie Flossie. What good would teeth be if there was nobody to tend the Fire and keep the Celestial Balance working, and bottle Kindness, and...."

"It's too late for your sappy sweetness. None of that matters anymore. Now everybody is going to know who I am. Now everybody will listen."

Little Wings didn't know what to think. "What do you mean?" she asked hesitatingly.

"The time has come. I'm going to prove to you that you're wrong and I'm right. It's time to destroy the Isle of Kindness. Then, as it spins deliciously out of control, the whole universe will know the power of Starling Patch. For I can do deeds that NO ONE can match!" Starling backed away howling and shrieking, consumed by the insanity of

a joke only he understood.

"But you never really win when you do something bad," cried Little Wings, and she ran to the bars and grabbed hold of them. She pulled at them with all her strength, trying to make them give way. "No, Starling, come back. You can't do that. Please! Come back!

"Oh, no," Little Wings cried, "I've done it again."

The Battle

But Starling Patch didn't even hear the Tooth Fairy's pleading cries. His mind was so full of hate as he left his cavity that he could hear nothing but his own evil laughter. The laughter grew louder and harsher as his seething hatred produced an unending row of evil duplicates that screeched and slinked across the icy terrain in a wide circle around the Isle of Kindness.

At the same time, near the base of the Eternal Fire, Blinker finished giving his final instructions to the Metrognomes.

"Okay, does everybody understand what to do?" he boomed. The Metrognomes nodded in unison. Blinker turned to Auntie Flossie, who stood beside him. "Everything's ready here, Ma'am."

"I hope this works," said Auntie Flossie. "I want this whole business settled once and for all."

"What about Little Wings?" Piper asked.

"We're just going to have to hope she can take care of herself for a little while longer," said Auntie Flossie.

Blinker spoke up again. "How about you, Ma'am? Wouldn't it be better if you went out on a moonbeam for a while, where it's safe? I mean, things may get pretty rough here, what with people throwin' bottles and all."

"No, that's very kind of you, Blinker, but my place is here. The Eternal Fire is my responsibility. You just give me some bottles of Kindness, and I'll make sure it doesn't go out. And speaking of those bottles, I'd rather you didn't throw them or hit

anyone with them."

"But, Auntie Flossie, they're our only weapons," cried Piper.

"Well, then, splash them or pour it on any Patches you see, but don't hurt anyone. It's the Touch of Kindness that's important, not conking people on the head!"

Suddenly, a cry rang out through the air like an alarm.

"IT'S PATCH!"

An army of identical soldiers closed in on the Eternal Fire from all sides. Rows and rows of Starling Patches, each armed with snowballs, marched slowly, side by side, closing the distance between themselves and the Fire.

Without wasting a blink, Blinker leaped to the top of the Celestial Balance with a bottle in each hand. His voice echoed out to all his Metrognomes.

"BOTTLE STATIONS!"

Metrognomes ran as quickly as they could to their posts at the fringe of the ice. Everybody was very busy, but there was little confusion. Every Metrognome knew exactly where to go. Auntie Flossie looked detemined as she stood by the Fire. They waited for the attack.

Blinker could see everything from where he stood. He called down to Piper and Ack. "Okay, Diaper. You two go out there and confuse them. Run around and make noise. Make them chase you. Just don't get caught. We'll do the rest."

"Let's go," Piper called to Ack.

The two scooted out onto the ice. Ack ran as fast as he could towards a column of Patches. As he skidded to a halt, he sent a huge spray

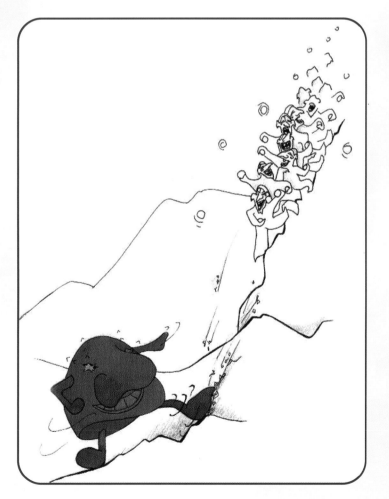

of ice into their faces, and they had to stop and wipe their eyes. When they did, the closest Metrognomes threw cupped handfuls of Kindness on them. They were still wiping their eyes as they disappeared with the sound of a bursting balloon. When Piper saw that, he couldn't have been happier. Then everything happened at once. Ack was running around, in and out between Metrognomes, with Patches trying to stop him, and Metrognomes were bombarding the Patches with Kindness. Pop! Pop! Pop! Every time the least bit of Kindness landed on a Patch... POP... he disappeared. Blinker doused them when they came near the Celestial Balance, Auntie Flossie sprinkled them when they approached the Eternal Fire, and Piper and Ack kept them confused. Everywhere there was noise. Piper was yelling and teasing the enemy, Blinker was shouting commands, and Patches were screaming, spitting and popping into thin air.

Suddenly, Piper noticed that the gruesome soldiers of evil were vanishing without even being touched by Kindness. Pop, pop, pop went the Patches. They were all mysteriously disappearing as Piper and Ack ran back to the Fire. Then, a horrible scream made everybody stop short and look around. There, jumping up and down on the ice was the last Starling Patch of all, shaking his fists with rage.

"NOoooooo!" he screamed. "You don't play fair. I'm supposed to win. Why can't I win? Nobody ever lets me win. Little Wings was right again. But I'm going to get her this time. I'm going to get her for good." And with that, Starling ran away in quick, short steps, every few feet, leaping high into the air.

Piper didn't even stop to think. He knew exactly what he had to do. He ran over to one of the cases of ammunition and took out two bottles.

"Here," he called to Ack, as he tossed him a bottle, "you might need one of these. Now let's go save Little Wings." Then Piper and his Sniffen friend darted back out onto the chilling ice.

Piper knew he had to keep Starling Patch in sight if they were ever to find Little Wings in time. At least, they knew she was still alive. But Starling was planning to do something disgustingly nasty, and they had to catch up to him. They couldn't afford to make a wrong turn. Suddenly, after one spectacular high leap into the air, Starling disappeared down into a hole in the icy ground.

"That must be his cavity," Piper yelled, pointing ahead. "I'll bet Little Wings is in there."

Piper Confronts Patch

Starling had gotten madder and madder with every step he had taken. Now the evil Metrognome was in his domain, and his rage was ready to erupt. Breathing heavily through the sides of his mouth, Patch stomped over to the frigid cell where Little Wings was a prisoner. When he looked at her, his hate suddenly exploded like a volcano. He swung both arms to one side, and with a mighty sweep, shattered six of the thick icicles that served as bars. Splinters of ice covered the floor to the gloomy cavity. The Tooth Fairy was on the opposite side of the jail cell, huddled against the bars. She was so cold, she could hardly move.

"It's out into the Consuming Colors with you, where you'll vanish forever!" Starling screamed at Little Wings. "Just like they wanted to do to me." And as he spoke, Starling grabbed the Tooth Fairy roughly. Then he threw her over his shoulder like a sack, holding onto her feet. He turned, spitting and growling, and ran back up and out of his frozen cavern. Just as Starling crawled out onto the icy surface, Piper reached the cavity entrance.

Once again, Patch was the first to react. Before Piper could even remember to use

the bottle he was holding, he felt a hard, cold hand on his forehead. Patch pushed Piper away with a shove so powerful that it sent the small boy tumbling backwards. Fortunately, he clutched the bottle of Kindness safely to his body, and it didn't break. Piper felt a bit dizzy. He looked around quickly for Ack.

"Ack, Ack, where are you?" Piper cried. "I need you." But the Sniffen was nowhere in sight, and Patch was on his way to the outer edge of the Isle. He couldn't worry about Ack. He had to save Little Wings.

Piper scrambled to his feet and ran after them. He gripped the bottle tightly as he approached the fiend. The flashes of light from the Consuming Colors cast a long dirty shadow from Patch's body across the ice towards Piper.

"Stop! Don't you come any closer, you little busybody," Patch screamed. "One more step and your dear, sweet little Tooth Fairy goes over the edge. Now, drop your weapon." Piper watched as Patch held Little Wings at arm's length over the mists of the Consuming Colors.

"Don't listen to him, Piper," said Little Wings, weak from prolonged exposure to the cold. "Forget about me. The important thing is to save the Isle of Kindness and all the people down on Earth."

"I mean it," Starling snarled. "Drop that bottle!" Piper couldn't do anything else. He didn't want anything to happen to the Tooth Fairy because of him. He placed the bottle gently on the ground beside his foot, so it wouldn't break. "Now, kick it over here," Starling ordered. "Nice and easy." Piper gave the bottle a slight nudge with his toes, and it went skittering across the glossy surface. Still holding Little Wings out over the misty edge, Starling bent down and picked up the bottle. His face twisted into a menacing grin.

"Thought you were pretty smart, didn't you," he shouted at Piper. "Well, who's the smart one now? Huh? It's Starling Patch!" He stepped away from the edge, still holding Little Wings tightly. "Now get over there where I can keep my eye on you," Starling commanded, pointing to the outer rim of the Isle. "If you want to get away, you can jump!" And with that, he opened his mouth wide and laughed like a hyena. Then he placed Little Wings' stiff, semi-conscious body onto the frozen ground, grasping her around the throat. He held the bottle right up to her nose.

"You know what this is? This is the niceness juice I had to bottle while you were out getting all the fame and glory. Only there's something I didn't know about this stuff. It makes you disappear." Little Wings looked up sadly at her captor, not knowing what to think of his words. "Oh, you didn't know that, either, eh?" he said. "Well, it does. They used it on my men when I tried to attack the Fire. As soon as they were touched by Kindness, they vanished." Patch moved in a little closer. "And now, you know what I'm going to have the pleasure of doing with this? I'm going to pour it all over you, and you're going to disappear, too, POP, just like they did." Starling looked over at Piper to make sure he stayed where he was. Then, he slowly worked the cap off of the bottle with his fangs and spat it out into the Consuming Colors.

Now Piper was almost certainly positively sure that nothing bad was going to happen when the Kindness was spilled onto Little Wings. And he was also just as convinced that Little Wings knew the same thing. Perhaps they could use that knowledge to turn the tables on Starling. If another of his evil plans failed, he might be so enraged that they could surprise him and take him prisoner. It was worth a try.

The Kindness must have dripped down onto Little Wings, although Piper couldn't see a drop of anything come out of the bottle. Little Wings wiggled and wriggled. She felt as if she were sitting in a bath of warm honey, only she didn't feel all sticky and icky. Starling stepped back to watch her pop. But the only sound he heard was the humming beat of her wings. Little Wings looked radiant and totally frostless. The Kindness had returned her warmth, and she flew revitalized into the air. Starling's latest failure was too much for him to take. He started screaming and jumping up and down in an uncontrollable temper tantrum.

"AAAAAHHHHH! STOP, STOP, STOP. YOU'RE SUPPOSED TO POP! WHY CAN'T I WIN? I WANT TO WIN!" Seeing that Starling was overcome by feeling sorry for himself, Piper decided to take advantage of the situation. He ran with all his might at Starling's legs, going in for a low tackle.

"Bad people never really win," Piper yelled. "Get him, Little Wings!"

Just as Piper slammed his shoulder into Starling Patch's legs, Little Wings flew at him from the rear, pushing him forward so he fell on his face. The three of them wrestled on the ground. Arms, legs and wings went every which way. And, though he was struggling with all his might, Piper felt Starling slowly begin to overpower them. Soon, with Little Wings and Piper in headlocks, one under each of his arms, Starling rose triumphantly from the ground.

Ack To The Rescue

Suddenly, "ACK" rang out loudly from behind one of the jagged piles of ice at the opening of Patch's cavity. Starling stopped struggling for a second, but it was a second too long. Out charged Ack the Sniffen with determination on his face and a bottle of Kindness in his hand.

Ack ran right up to Starling's feet and kicked him in the shins as hard as he could. Starling screamed in pain and released his hold on Little Wings and Piper. Piper fell to the ground and rolled off to one side. Little Wings felt herself falling, so she flapped her wings at top speed, to break her fall. Patch was so angry as his shins throbbed with pain that his only thought was to get even with Ack.

Howling with rage, he lunged at the little fellow, his eyes burning with hatred. This time, however, Ack was too fast for Starling, and with an underhand motion, he splashed Kindness right in the villain's ugly face, catching him in mid-lunge. The bully froze instantly in a horrifying monster pose. But he didn't pop. He only stopped — Evil encased in ice.

The Melting

"Ack, Ack, you did it!" Piper yelled happily, and ran over to the smiling Sniffen. Little Wings flew down and threw her arms around Ack. Soon, they were jumping around and dancing in a circle, totally unaware of the cold and ice around them. Suddenly, Piper stopped because he heard voices in the distance. He turned towards the center of the Isle and stood in wonder.

The ice was slowly receding, and the silver and gold flames of the Eternal Fire were hopping higher and brighter than Piper had ever seen them. As the ice withdrew more and more, the sadness and frost were replaced with happiness and warmth. What Piper had thought were round hills of ice were really sparkling domes of every color imaginable. They were all connected by paths of the same colors. Piper saw Auntie Flossie, Blinker and several Metrognomes, including the now unfrozen Tapper, running on the paths towards them. Little Wings waved gaily to them, as Ack grinned broadly.

"What happened to Patch," Blinker asked.

"He's frozen solid," Little Wings answered.

"But what will happen to him when the ice melts?" Piper asked worriedly. "I mean, if Tapper's thawed out, maybe Starling will, too."

"Hmmm, we better get close to him and check it," said Blinker. And just as they reached the iced-over villain, the melting began.

Ice disappeared slowly from Starling's toes to his legs, climbed up to his arms, and delicately vanished from around his fingers. Then it thawed from the top of his arms, leaving his chest free of ice, and then clearing his face of icicles and frost. The trail of melting ice slowly inched down his back from head to heel, and crept away softly on to the edge of the Isle.

Starling still didn't move. Was he pretending to be frozen so he could surprise everyone? No, nobody could hold a position like that for so long. And the funny thing was, he no longer seemed very mean. With the hanging ice off his face, he wasn't bad looking at all!

The Isle of Kindness was now a sparkling carnival of colors. As he looked around at the Isle, and then out at the flashing wisps of light that surrounded it, Piper felt as if he were standing in the center of a dazzling circular rainbow. It was truly beautiful.

Everyone moved cautiously around what had once been a very active and evil Metrognome.

"I wonder why he didn't disappear," Blinker pondered as he blinked at the statue-like form of Starling Patch.

"I imagine it's because Starling's hate was so great," replied Auntie Flossie, "that concentrated Kindness could only stop it. It couldn't make it go away entirely."

"Well, what do you think we should do with him?" Blinker asked, scratching his head. "Should we throw him over the side as we were going to do in the beginning?" The Metrognomes looked at each other, trying to decide what to do. Then the Tooth Fairy flew over to Blinker.

A Special Kiss

"Blinker," she said softly, "I know it was all my fault that this happened. But, even after all he did to me, I think I was right all along. And I have another idea. Maybe we didn't use the right type of Kindness on Starling. I want you all to get around him in a circle so he has no chance to escape. If this doesn't work, you can do whatever you think is best."

The Tooth Fairy moved her wings, and slowly flew upward until she was right beside Starling's stony face. Her eyes twinkled with life. Without the slightest hesitation, Little Wings leaned in and kissed Starling on the cheek.

Everything was quiet as Little Wings flew back to Ack's side. Everyone looked on intently, without even breathing.

Then Patch moved. In a wave of relaxation, his whole body eased into a more natural, non-menacing posture. As he stood up, every Metrognome was alert, watching, ready to grab him. Starling looked over quickly at all who surrounded him. He licked his lips nervously.

(SONG: "I'm Sorry")

Sighs of relief came from the circle. Metrognomes grinned and smiled at Little Wings, whose eyes sparkled with joy. Finally, she had done something right.

Yet, amidst all that happiness, there was one sad face. Starling hung his head and, dragging his feet, walked over to Auntie Flossie. He couldn't look into her eyes as he spoke.

"I am truly sorry, Ma'am," he said quietly, "for causing so much trouble. I think it would be best for everybody if I just left."

"I know how you must feel," Auntie Flossie said understandingly, "but where would you go?"

"Out into the Consuming Colors, where I belong."

Blinker moved forward and extended his hand. "Don't be silly, Patcher. It's good to have you back again the way you were. Besides, we need you. My work clothes are going to need a mending soon, and you're the only one who knows how to do it. And you're still welcome on the bottle crew if you'd like to share the shift work with the others. Here, shake on it!"

With a puzzled look, Patcher shook hands with Blinker. "But, I don't understand," he said. "How can you just...?"

"What kind of people would we be," interrupted Auntie Flossie, "if we weren't able to forgive those who know they've been wrong? You said you were sorry, didn't you?"

"Yes, I did. And I meant it, too."

"Then it's settled." Auntie Flossie smiled. "Welcome back, Patcher."

Piper leaned over to Little Wings. "Why is everyone calling Starling 'Patcher' now?" he asked. The Tooth Fairy didn't have a chance to answer.

"Because that used to be my name before I got bad and changed it," said Patcher, moving over towards them. "I used to be the official mender around here. And I guess I am again, come to think of it!" Piper shook hands and introduced himself. Then Patcher looked at Ack and Little Wings. He took a deep breath and swallowed before he spoke.

"I guess I was wrong about a lot of things," he said. "I should have been proud of my name and my job. I had it pretty good around here, but it took you two to show me. Thanks to you, the evil Starling Patch is dead and gone forever." And then Patcher leaned over, and with the gentlest motion in the universe, he bowed deeply. "Thank you, Little Wings," he said.

Then he kneeled down to Ack. "And thank you, Ack." The little Sniffen grinned and stuck out his sticklike hand. Patcher laughed, shook hands, and stood up. He turned to all those watching him. "Let's give three cheers to the Tooth Fairy and her two little friends!"

(SONG: "Three Cheers")

"Come on, " Blinker bellowed, "let's get back to work! We've got Kindness to bottle."

The Touch Of Kindness

As Blinker, Auntie Flossie and the Metrognomes headed back towards the Fire, Patcher held out his hands to Little Wings and Piper. They each took one of his hands, and the three started down a silver and gold path towards the Eternal Fire with Ack skipping along happily ahead of them.

"These domes are where we all live," said Patcher. He nodded towards the one on the left. "My mending shop is that blue one right over there."

"Wow, what a wonderful place this is," Piper said to Little Wings when they got back to the Celestial Balance. "I wish I could stay here forever."

"But, I'm afraid that's impossible, Piper," said Auntie Flossie, coming up to him. "You have a home and a family down on Earth, and that's where you belong."

"I know, Auntie Flossie, you're right," Piper agreed sadly, "but I hate leaving friends, and I'll miss you all very much. I've had a good time, and I'm glad I could help after all.

There's just one thing that I can't do that I wish I could."

"What's that?" Auntie Flossie asked.

"See Kindness like the rest of you can," Piper answered.

"You wait until you get home, Piper," Auntie Flossie continued. "Seeing the color isn't the important part. You'll be able to feel it all around you. And where you don't feel it, try to put some. Be nice to others. Help them out. It's been there all along, Piper. You just never thought to look for it. It's like us. It took you to show us that bottles of Kindness could defeat the evil that was choking the Isle and putting out the Fire. You know, sometimes we overlook the most obvious solutions.

(SONG: "The Touch of Kindness")

"Now, say goodbye to everyone," Auntie Flossie said quietly. "I'm afraid it's time for me to take you home."

Goodbye

Auntie Flossie waited as Piper moved among the busy Metrognomes, shaking hands and saying goodbye. He climbed the ladder leading to Blinker's foreman's perch.

"Thanks for everything, Blinker," Piper said.

"That's okay, Diaper," said Blinker. "You've been real helpful. And if you're ever back here again, bring some of that wood with you. I'd like to see it. And remember...

(REPRISE OF SONG: "It's All Right If Your Teeth Fall Out")

"You take care, Diaper."

Piper smiled and waved goodbye and scampered quickly down the ladder, looking for Ack. The little Sniffen was over at the Kindness Tap, capping bottles as fast as Napper could fill them.

"Hey, Ack, come here." Ack ran over to Piper with quick, short steps. "You're really a part of things now, aren't you?" Piper said. Ack's face broke into a broad smile, and he nodded. "Well, I wanted to say goodbye, Ack. I'm glad you were with us out there on the ice. You're a good lookout, and a wonderful friend... and you cap bottles well, too!" Piper gave Ack a final wave and turned to go off to find Little Wings.

He didn't have very far to go, for as he turned, there she was. She stood there looking at him with that same cute expression on her face, her little wings vibrating slightly. They just looked at each other for a few seconds without knowing what to say. Piper spoke up first.

"I don't think we should say goodbye, Little Wings, 'cause good friends always keep in touch with one another, and I think we've become really good friends in a very short time. Besides, I've still got two teeth that haven't come out, and they'll be getting loose very soon."

Little Wings looked over at Auntie Flossie to make sure she hadn't heard anything. Then she gave Piper a wink, leaned over, and kissed him lightly on the cheek.

Sometimes, leaving friends is a very hard thing to do, and it gets difficult to see through the tears in your eyes. But, somehow, Piper found his way back to the Landing Station.

"I'm ready to go now, Auntie Flossie," he said softly.

(SONG: "Goodbye to Piper")

Piper wanted the trip back home to last a long time, but he knew that was impossible. Trips home always seem shorter somehow! As he rode the moonbeam back to Earth, he waved to everyone on the Isle of Kindness until they became too small to see. Soon, Auntie Flossie was lifting him up onto his window sill, and thanking him for his help. His trip to where the Tooth Fairies live had come to an end.

Piper walked behind his bed and got into his pajamas. Then he remembered. They forgot his tooth! He jumped into bed and grabbed the pillow. There, next to a piece of string, was the shiniest coin he had ever seen. He was so amazed and happy all at once, that he giggled joyously as if someone were tickling him. Then he propped his pillow back against the headboard and lay down with his hands behind his head. He stared out of his window into the twinkling heavens.

As he slowly fell asleep, Piper knew, without question, that no matter what he did later on in his life, he would make sure there was a lot more Kindness in the world for a long time to come.

CD SET ARTISTS

ORCHESTRA

Piano/Arranger/Conductor - Richard Iacona
Bass - Mike Hall
Drums - Tony Tedesco
Guitar - Ron Affif
Synthesizer - Michael Tornick

CAST/SINGERS

Narrator - John Arthur Long
Little Wings, the Tooth Fairy - Anastasia Kastrinos
Piper Noble - Catherine Stephani
Ack, the Sniffen - Molly Greenblatt
Auntie Flossie - Phyllis March
"You Can Ride On A Moonbeam" soloist - Dana Zenobi
Blinker - Steve Diamant/John Arthur Long
Starling Patch - John Arthur Long
Chorus: Danielle Bellini, Josh Diamant, Jeff Eisner, Brenda Festo
Joe Lynch, Thomas March, Gina Mattia, Lisa Padula,
Carly Sperber, Alana Wolfe

AUDIO PRODUCTION

E.S.P. Studios
Anthony D'Erasmo, Engineer